# From A to Zamboni

## The Alphabet, Hockey Style!

Written by

## Jennifer Grocki

Illustrated by

## Andy Lendway

# From A to Zamboni©
## The Alphabet, Hockey Style!

Team Kidz Inc.

P.O. Box 2111

Voorhees, NJ 08043

ISBN 10: 0-9793833-0-7

ISBN 13: 978-0-9793833-0-4

# Dedication

In loving memory of my mother Judy, who had a passion for life,
literature, and hockey, and to my niece Lilly and nephew Jack
in hopes that they follow in her footsteps.

- JG

For my wife Laura and my daughter Cally, who support me in everything.
Thanks to Mom and Dad, who always told me I could be anything I wanted
as long as I was happy.
I am!

- AL

A portion of the proceeds will benefit

www.comcastspectacorfoundation.org

**A** is for **A**nthem, we sing with great pride,

B is for Bench, where we sit side by side.

C is for Coach, who stands tall and proud,

**D** is for **D**efense, through which no goal's allowed.

E is for Elbows, that can't get too high,

F is for Fans, who watch us fly by.

G is for Goalie, who guards our team's net,

H is for High stick, we'll never forget.

I is for Ice, we can't play without,

J is for Jersey, worn with honor, no doubt.

K is for Kicking, we know we can't do,

L is for Linesman, whose eyes are on you.

**M** is for **Mask**, which we wear on our face,

N is for Net, where the puck finds its place.

O is for Obstruction, which gets you the door,

P is for Puck, we pass, shoot, and we score!

Q is for Quiet, when we don't have the lead,

R is for Red Line, we cross with great speed.

S is for Stick, we handle with care,

T is for Team, who will always be there.

U is for Underdog, which we've all been before,

**V is for Victory, the moment we score!**

W is for Winger, who avoids a big fight,

X is for X-ray, often needed each night.

Y is for Yippee, you yell with a friend,

**Z** is for **Z**amboni machine, making ice at **The End!**

# Autographs

# Autographs